OUT
SIDE

OUTSIDE
BY PAUL DUNN

PLAYWRIGHTS CANADA PRESS
TORONTO

LIBRARY AND ARCHIVES CANADA CATALOGUING IN PUBLICATION
Dunn, Paul, author
    Outside / Paul Dunn. -- First edition.

A play.
Issued in print and electronic formats.
ISBN 978-1-77091-810-8 (softcover).--ISBN 978-1-77091-811-5 (PDF).
--ISBN 978-1-77091-812-2 (HTML).--ISBN 978-1-77091-813-9 (Kindle)

    I. Title.

PS8607.U552O98 2017   jC812'.6   C2017-904518-0
                                          C2017-904519-9

We acknowledge the financial support of the Canada Council for the Arts, the Ontario Arts Council (OAC), the Ontario Media Development Corporation and the Government of Canada for our publishing activities.

 Canada Council Conseil des arts
for the Arts du Canada

 **ONTARIO ARTS COUNCIL**
CONSEIL DES ARTS DE L'ONTARIO
an Ontario government agency
un organisme du gouvernement de l'Ontario

 Canadä

 Ontario
Ontario Media Development
Corporation

For Andrew Lamb and Roseneath Theatre:
the fearless and tireless champions of this play.

Outside was developed through Roseneath Theatre's TYA Playwrights Unit. It was originally produced by Roseneath Theatre in April 2015, and was remounted in March 2016 and January 2017 with the following cast and creative team:

Daniel: G. Kyle Shields
Krystina: Mina James
Jeremy: Youness Aladdin (2015) / Giacomo Sellar (2016–2017)

Directed by Andrew Lamb
Dramatruged by Rosemary Rowe
Stage managed by Maureen Callaghan (2015) / Meghan Speakman (2016) / Krista MacIsaac (2017)
Set designed by Michael Greves
Costumes designed by Lindsay C. Walker
Sound designed by Verne Good

Managing Director: Natalie Ackers / Annemieke Wade
Production Manager: Heather Landon / Courtney Pyke
Education and Marketing: Gretel Meyer Odell, Katya Kuznetsova, Victoria Augustynek, Nan Chen, and Brittany Kay
Tour Manager: Niki Poirier / Nicole Myers

Outside was developed through support from Roseneath Theatre, the Ontario Arts Council Theatre Creators' Reserve and Theatre Direct.

CHARACTERS

Daniel—sweet, intelligent and poetic. Fifteen.

Krystina—kick-ass and super smart. Fifteen.

Jeremy—athletic, down-to-earth, funny and dry. Fifteen.

NOTES

A forward slash (/) in the text indicates an overlap.

When performing the play in a country other than Canada, the reference to Louis Riel (and the rap) may be changed to a suitable local historical figure, with the permission of and consultation with the playwright.

SETTING

Outside takes place in two separate classrooms in two separate high schools during the course of a single lunch hour.

Two classrooms, each in a separate school. One classroom is in Salisbury Collegiate, where KRYSTINA and JEREMY will be meeting, and the other is in an unnamed school, where DANIEL is speaking to us. Both classrooms exist simultaneously, and the focus shifts between the two.

At Salisbury Collegiate, KRYSTINA is attempting to hang a large, hand-painted rainbow banner across the blackboard. It is proving to be tricky. Painted on the banner are the words "Salisbury Collegiate GSA." Standing on a chair, she tapes the right side up, and then she gets down and moves the chair over to the left side. Just as she is managing to tape the left side up, the right side falls—

KRYSTINA   No no no no crap not AGAIN!

She slumps into the chair in frustration. A lunch bell. We hear the sounds of students moving through the halls, lockers opening and closing—shouts, laughter, etc. KRYSTINA goes to the classroom door, and with a deep breath opens it. She catches the eye of someone in the hall and tentatively waves.

At the other school, DANIEL settles into his chair and addresses us, as if we are the other students at a lunchtime meeting with him.

DANIEL Hi, yeah. Um . . . hi. I'm Daniel. You guys know that. Or maybe some of you don't. I've been at this school two months and I've barely said a word. Not 'cause I don't like you guys or anything, I'm just . . . none of you know why I'm here, why I transferred here, I mean. Ms. Franjelica knows, 'cause she was part of getting me here so that I could be, um, "safe," which is why she let me take over today's meeting so that I could ask you guys if . . .

KRYSTINA and DANIEL each take a deep breath, together. KRYSTINA turns back to the banner, approaching it with renewed resolve, as DANIEL braves on—

I'm wondering if you could do me a favour. See, at my old school I still have two friends . . . Krystina and Jeremy. They are trying to start a club like this one. A Gay-Straight Alliance. They're both, um, straight, but they're all right, if you know what I mean. And I'm betting they don't have a lot of support.

JEREMY bursts into the classroom KRYSTINA is in. He is in his soccer gear.

KRYSTINA Jeremy! You're here!

JEREMY   I'm here.

KRYSTINA   I thought you had practice.

JEREMY   Oh, we do, but I couldn't concentrate. I kept thinking of you, here, trying to do this . . . and, and how Daniel's gone. That was the best answer they could come up with. To transfer him. I'm out on the field trying to get better, as a, a . . . teammate for this school, and all I can think is . . . my school . . . *blows*. So I just walked off the field. Right in the middle of drills.

KRYSTINA   Wow.

JEREMY   Coach is pissed. And when I told him where I was going, he called after me, "When I was a kid we didn't need special clubs. We toughed it out."

Beat.

KRYSTINA   Well. Welcome.

JEREMY   *(looks around)* Where's everyone else, Krystina?

KRYSTINA   This is it. You and me.

JEREMY   Huh.

He sees the banner.

Bit much, don't you think?

KRYSTINA   I spent hours painting that.

JEREMY   Okay then.

They wait.

DANIEL   Oh jeez . . . talking is hard. I would so much rather just listen to you guys. I remember my first meeting, when you were all complaining about your class schedules, just complaining about school, and it took half the meeting before the word "queer" even came up, and I was like . . . I was in heaven. And I know it's not like . . . "Hey, this is the club where we sit around and talk about our GAY PAIN," 'cause who'd wanna go to that, really, but some of you have shared about stuff that's been hard for you, and that has helped me more than you could know, and so . . . I would like to tell you my story. I'm ready. Right, Ms. F?

Beat.

She's nodding, so, where to begin . . .

DANIEL takes a deep breath.

JEREMY   We should've offered free pizza or something. To get people to come.

KRYSTINA   Then people would just come for the pizza. We don't want that.

JEREMY   Don't we want people to come?

KRYSTINA   Yes, but that's not the point.

JEREMY Oh-kaaay . . . Do people know what room we're in?

KRYSTINA Miss Gibbons made an announcement.

JEREMY When?

KRYSTINA This morning, before the bell.

JEREMY Right, like anyone heard that.

KRYSTINA I put posters up, in the caf.

JEREMY I didn't see any.

KRYSTINA On the board.

JEREMY There weren't any, Krystina. I walked by there between first and second period. Maybe they got torn down.

KRYSTINA You know what, fine, this is stupid.

JEREMY What?

KRYSTINA No one's coming, that's obvious.

JEREMY No, hey, hey—just wait a minute. I didn't mean . . . maybe people just don't wanna, I don't know . . . seem eager?

    Beat.

    Here, let's . . . um . . .

He goes to the banner and tries to fix it. KRYS-
TINA eventually joins him.

DANIEL   Right. Got it. Middle school. Where dreams come true. Ha. I'm sitting on the school bus with these girls who were my friends, 'cause I've always had girls as friends. And we're listening to that song, you know the one by that super trashy pop star who, like, won that competition and then had that one song about, well, doing it? *(sings)* "I wanna do it, do it, do it, all niiiiight, with yoooooou"—and my friends are imitating her, kinda trying to sing like her and kinda making fun of her at the same time. We're laughing so hard, and then Joni says, "Make Daniel sing it. He sings it the best." Which was true. Joni's begging me to do it, and her friends are now begging me to do it, and so I do it—I sing it and it is . . . awesome, and it fills the bus . . . and then . . . silence. And then Jared, who I'd just met that year, at the start of grade seven, who was way too tall for his age and looked like someone stretched him overnight, sitting at the back of the bus, he says, "Hey, Daniel, are you a faggot?" He asks it like he's genuinely curious about it. Cutting through the silence of that bus, from way at the back, "Hey, Daniel, are you a faggot?"

Beat.

It becomes a game after that. Some kid stops me in the hall, asks me do I know the way to the music room, and I say, "Sure, that way," and then he says oh yeah and can he ask me something else? And I say sure, and he says, "Are you a faggot?" And then I notice the group waiting, just down the hall, watching us and already laughing . . . or I'm in the cafeteria and some kid is sitting beside me and we start a conversation; we talk for five, ten minutes and I'm thinking, "This is nice," and then she says, "Cool. And are you a faggot?" The game was to catch me off guard. They created a point system and kept score. New students would do it as a rite of passage. So I was like, fine, then I won't talk to anyone, I swear. I'd walk to school repeating to myself, "Just keep your mouth shut, keep your mouth shut." But I would fall for it, every time. Try not talking to anyone for a whole day, not once. Maybe some of you have? And now some of you are looking at me like, "This is the part where you told someone, right?" Nope. I felt that if I did I would be making it into a big deal; I would be making it real, what was happening, and I didn't want it to be real. Who wants to be that guy? No. Forget it. I just did my best to . . . not think about it . . . I was like, okay, I've messed up junior high for myself, royally, but it'll change in high school, because I'll smarten up before then, and there'll be lots of new kids from other middle schools there, and a lot of *these* kids will go to different high schools, right? I'll get a clean start when I get to Salisbury Collegiate. You guys know that school? One district over . . .

KRYSTINA   I always wanted to start a club, you know?

JEREMY   Yeah? Well now you have. A big gay club.

They wait—their enthusiasm waning.

Check us out.

DANIEL   Compared to my middle school, Salisbury Collegiate is massive. It's so big. Which might be scary if you're another kid, but for me I was like, "All right, let's *blend in.*" I was hoping to just disappear, you know? In the sea of new faces. *"Daniel who?"* That would suit me just fine. I didn't know anyone in my grade nine homeroom. Sweet. I sit still. I keep my head down. I keep my *mouth shut.* Krystina and Jeremy were in my homeroom too, with Mr. Mercer, who taught us social studies.

JEREMY   I blame you.

KRYSTINA   Why?

DANIEL   We were thrown together for a project.

JEREMY   No way would I be sitting in this empty room at lunch if you hadn't picked me for your stupid history group.

DANIEL   One day, Mercer calls out "groups of three," and before I know it, Krystina, who sits in front of me, whips around and says—

   A shift/flashback—DANIEL, KRYSTINA and JEREMY are back in their homeroom.

KRYSTINA   You and me.

DANIEL   Me?

KRYSTINA Yeah, and . . . *(points to JEREMY)* him.

JEREMY What?

KRYSTINA You got a problem with that?

JEREMY No, just . . . don't you usually like to work with . . . um . . .

DANIEL Brianna and Carmen?

JEREMY Yeah, them.

KRYSTINA Sure, I'd be happy to work with them if they were interested in, you know, *learning.* Apparently school's too hard for Carmen now that she has boobs.

JEREMY Yeah.

KRYSTINA You guys are friends, right?

DANIEL &
JEREMY No.

JEREMY Umm . . .

KRYSTINA Oh.

DANIEL I don't think we've ever really spoken. Hi.

JEREMY Yeah, hi.

KRYSTINA But you sit right next to each other.

The boys shrug.

'Kay, whatever, so what do you want to do?

JEREMY   What's the assignment?

**KRYSTINA
& DANIEL**   Louis Riel.

JEREMY   Right.

DANIEL   How about, I don't know . . . like a music video.

JEREMY   That's so gay.

Beat.

KRYSTINA   Are you a jerk, Jeremy?

JEREMY   What? No.

KRYSTINA   Then don't talk like one. A music video. That's one idea, thank you, Daniel. Let's continue to brainstorm.

She pulls out a piece of paper from her binder, pen poised.

We could write a play. Or like a comedy sketch.

JEREMY snorts.

DANIEL   Yeah. I like that.

KRYSTINA   You could contribute something, Jeremy, instead of knocking everything down.

JEREMY   Yeah, sure, I got ideas, whatever.

DANIEL   Or a graphic novel thing. Louis Riel as like a superhero. Jeremy's a really good drawer.

JEREMY   What?

DANIEL   I've seen him. In art class.

KRYSTINA   Great.

She writes it down.

JEREMY   Or, like, a rap song.

DANIEL   Yeah, that's original.

JEREMY   What?

DANIEL   Oh my god, a *rap song*? There will be, like, ten terrible rap songs. I'll bet you anything.

KRYSTINA   He's right. That's a really terrible idea, Jeremy.

DANIEL   Yeah. Really terrible.

JEREMY   Shut up!

DANIEL   *(beat-boxing and rapping, badly)* My name's Louis Riel, and I'm here to *say*, Métis people are here to *stay* . . .

JEREMY   'Kay, whatever. I get it.

*Back to the two separate classrooms. DANIEL
addresses us.*

DANIEL   And I'm like, what's happening here, am I making . . .
friends? Shut up. No way. 'Kay, Daniel, play it cool,
don't *eff it up*. Right? We never would have hung out
otherwise, and it was a big project that we had to
work on over weeks and weeks. I wasn't expecting
BFFs from those guys—I wasn't expecting anything.
But wow, it felt good.

Beat.

Jeremy wouldn't talk to me, out there, outside, in the
world beyond our project, but it wasn't 'cause he was
being a jerk, he just . . . he had his teammates and his
own . . . whatever, but he would nod at me in the hallway, and Krystina began to pass me notes in class. She
had us over to her house, to work. One time, Jeremy
was late and so we spent an hour bitching about
Carmen and Brianna. We hung out, even when we
weren't doing homework, we'd take the bus into the
city, and see plays and movies at the rep cinema, and
suddenly I'm like, yay! I have a life! I start to relax, to
enjoy my time at Salisbury Collegiate, and then . . .
And then.

Beat.

I'm standing in the cafeteria at lunch, and my phone, which I barely use, starts buzzing in my backpack. It's a . . . text. "Are you still a faggot?"

KRYSTINA   As I was painting that banner, the door was open to the hall, and these girls saw me and they shouted at me as they passed.

JEREMY   What'd they shout?

KRYSTINA   I don't want to say.

JEREMY   C'mon, what'd they call you?

KRYSTINA   "Dyke!"

JEREMY   That's original.

DANIEL   "Are you still a faggot?" I look up and I can't tell where it's coming from, who sent it. I'm standing there, sweating, spinning around, trying to see who's watching me, who's laughing, but the cafeteria is packed and I can't tell.

JEREMY   Who was it?

KRYSTINA   Niners. Mocked by niners. They're the new kids and yet they're calling me a name.

JEREMY   Report it.

KRYSTINA   Mr. Williams was standing right there.

JEREMY   What?

KRYSTINA   Yeah.

JEREMY   And he heard?

KRYSTINA   He sort of called after them—they were already way down the hall—he was like, "Hey...hey girls..." but they didn't hear him, and so he turned and looked at me and sort of shrugged like, "Well, I tried, but you know, what do you expect?" And then he came over and closed the door. "Maybe just keep this closed for now, while there's a lot of traffic in the hall," and I said "thanks." I can't believe it, I said thanks...

KRYSTINA moves to the door, peering out.

DANIEL   *(slowly, considering)* "Are you still a faggot?" I started to get messages every day, sometimes many times a day. I don't know how they got my number. My phone was new—my parents got it for me over the summer. Not even a smartphone, a...It was supposed to be for me to call if I ever got into trouble, or for them to reach me in an emergency. When the next bill came in, they freaked—they had only bought the most basic plan; they wanted to know who was texting me all day long, and I lied, I said...my friends. I was afraid of that look on my dad's face. Sometimes he looks at me, and I can tell he's...scared...for me. Like he wishes I was...I wanted them to think that I was doing well at school. That I was okay. I...I paid for the texts out of my allowance and I begged them to get an all-inclusive plan. Because. I was determined to sort it out, you know? I would lay low and . . . contain it and it would eventually stop and then I could start all over. Right?

KRYSTINA   *(almost whispering, to JEREMY)* She's back.

JEREMY   Who?

KRYSTINA   The girl.

JEREMY   What girl?

KRYSTINA   No! Don't look!

JEREMY   Okay.

KRYSTINA   Short, with sorta spiky hair. She was out there before, hanging around, before you got here, like she wanted maybe to come in—

(calling out) Hi! We've started, but you can join us anytime.

JEREMY   *(to KRYSTINA)* We haven't started, no one's here.

KRYSTINA   *(to JEREMY)* We're here.

(to girl in the hall) Oh, you're not . . . what's that? Just hanging out, cool. Well so are we, so, *whatevs.* No *presh.*

JEREMY   You are so sad.

KRYSTINA   Shut up. Oh no. Now I've scared her away.

JEREMY   Is she a lesbian, though?

KRYSTINA   I don't know! And don't you dare ask her!

JEREMY   Why not? Isn't that the point of this? She tells us she's a lesbian and then we're all, "That's great! We'll be your friends! And help you out if someone's, like, bullying you or whatever . . . "

KRYSTINA just glares at him.

What!? Am I wrong?

KRYSTINA   IF she decides to come in here, the last thing I want is for you to put her on the spot by demanding to know how she identifies herself. IF she decides to come in here, and IF she feels comfortable sharing with us that she, at present, self-identifies as lesbian or bisexual or, or, queer or transgender or transsexual or, or even two-spirit or intersex or questioning—

JEREMY   Holy crap—

KRYSTINA   IF she reveals that to us, on her own terms and in her own time, then we offer our support—

JEREMY   Intersex, though? I don't even know what intersex is.

KRYSTINA   So look it up.

JEREMY   Why don't you just tell me.

KRYSTINA Because if you react in an immature or insensitive way I'll be really, really mad.

JEREMY Why, are you intersex?

KRYSTINA What did I just say about asking people!?

JEREMY Yeah, but you're *you* . . . I mean . . .

KRYSTINA Go over to that corner. Turn away. Look it up. And turn back when you're ready to talk about it.

> *JEREMY reluctantly obeys. He looks up intersex on his device.*

DANIEL I don't think Krystina knew. About the texting game. Some people seem to be exempt from the crap that's going on around them, 'cause the kids who are doing it know that they won't play along. Like everyone knows they're *good*. That's Krystina.

> *JEREMY turns around, unfazed.*

JEREMY You underestimate me.

KRYSTINA Yeah?

JEREMY Yeah. I'm . . . pretty progressive, you know. I'm here, aren't I?

KRYSTINA Yes.

JEREMY Tell me you're intersex if you're intersex—

KRYSTINA   I'm not.

JEREMY   Fine. But if you were I wouldn't care. I don't see why we need to be all precious about it. What if what that girl needs is for someone like me to just ask her point-blank if she's a lesbian, like it's no big deal, like I know tons of lesbians, because who knows, maybe I do, and it's aaalll cooooolll. And she can finally say, "You know what, yeah." And I save her the stress of having to come out.

KRYSTINA   How's she gonna know you're not asking her to make fun of her? How's she gonna know you're asking 'cause you care?

JEREMY   I don't know. Maybe because I'm sitting under this huge gay banner? Maybe because it's so, so gay in here?

KRYSTINA   I'm gonna kill you.

JEREMY   You can't afford to. You need me for your club.

KRYSTINA   And what if she's straight?

JEREMY doesn't know.

DANIEL   Jeremy, on the other hand, was a different story. A little more complicated.

JEREMY   So if we've started, let's start.

KRYSTINA   Really?

JEREMY   You got a plan, or something? You've obviously been doing your homework.

KRYSTINA   Yeah, but we should wait for . . . someone to . . . I mean it's a gay-straight alliance, and with just you and me—

JEREMY   I can't believe you're assuming that I'm straight. I thought this was a safe space, Krystina.

KRYSTINA   Jeremy—

JEREMY   You got a plan for this meeting? An "agenda"?

KRYSTINA   Of course I do.

JEREMY   Of course you do.

KRYSTINA goes and gets out a binder, flips . . .

KRYSTINA   We need to come up with a mission statement.

JEREMY   That sounds hard.

KRYSTINA   No . . . we can just start by talking about why we're here.

JEREMY   I think you should go first because you are the leader.

KRYSTINA   There's no leader. We can have a chairperson, if we want, but we have to elect—

JEREMY   Oh my god fine. I'll go. "Why am I here?"

KRYSTINA   Yes.

JEREMY   Well I'm here because . . . because Daniel's a good guy. And I don't like that he's gone.

KRYSTINA   Right.

JEREMY   And I guess I wish I had been better at . . . you know . . .

KRYSTINA   What?

JEREMY   Stuff.

　　　　　Beat.

KRYSTINA   "*Better at stuff* "!? Jeremy!

JEREMY   Well, like, for instance, there was this one time, early on, before things got so . . . you know—

DANIEL   Just as I was getting the hang of blocking numbers, and deleting texts without looking at them—

JEREMY   'Kay, so, you don't know this, and . . . and don't hate me . . .

KRYSTINA   Why would I hate you?

DANIEL   It took a step up. It's the end of the day. I'm heading toward the doors thinking, "I made it through another one," when I'm pushed into the lockers and informed that this is a "no fags hallway."

　　　　　Another shift/flashback. DANIEL is clutching his arm. JEREMY approaches him.

JEREMY   Hey, hey, Daniel. You okay?

DANIEL   Oh, look who's gonna risk talking to me. In public.

JEREMY   *(looking around quickly)* There's no one around.

DANIEL   I stand corrected.

JEREMY   They pushed you pretty hard.

DANIEL   Yeah, pushing. That's new.

JEREMY   You should watch out, maybe.

DANIEL   Oh, yeah, is that what I should do?

> *JEREMY begins to walk away. DANIEL calls after him.*

What am I doing? Jeremy?

JEREMY   What do you mean?

DANIEL   You've stopped acknowledging me in the hallway. When others are around. You used to nod. You used to do this— *(demonstrates)*

JEREMY   I can't, I'll get ...

DANIEL   What?

JEREMY   Look, our project is done, okay?

DANIEL   Yeah.

JEREMY   And you're . . .

DANIEL   What?

JEREMY   Oh c'mon, man. Don't act like you don't know.

DANIEL   I don't. What am I doing?

JEREMY   You know what people say about you.

DANIEL   And do you believe them?

> *JEREMY shrugs.*

But what am I doing?

JEREMY   I don't know . . . nothing, it's . . . Just, shoot . . . just look at yourself. It's just the way you are.

> *Back to the separate classrooms.*

DANIEL   Just the way I am, he says.

KRYSTINA   WHAT!?

JEREMY   I *know.* And he limped off . . . I wanted to help him, I really did, but I felt so . . . stuck. So, I'm here, I guess, because I wanna see if anyone else feels . . . stuck, like that. And maybe figure out how to get better at handling . . . that kind of . . . stuff.

Beat.

Yeah.

KRYSTINA That's . . .

JEREMY What, is that stupid?

KRYSTINA No. That's, um . . . right on.

She goes to her binder.

That's so right on I'm going to write that down.

JEREMY Sweet. Check me out.

KRYSTINA hands him a sheet of paper and a pen.

KRYSTINA And you too. Brainstorm. Reasons we need a club like this. As many as you can think of.

JEREMY 'Kay. One, two, three—go.

They brainstorm and write.

DANIEL Just the way I am. I go to the boys' washroom. I splash some water on my face. I stand at the mirror. I look at myself. I walk back and forth. I talk to myself, I say, "Hi." I still don't get it. So I say, "Fag, you're a faggot, are you a faggot? Huh? It's just the way you are." I'm looking in the mirror and that's when I . . . see it. I see what they see. And I think, damn, that kid needs to step it up. That kid needs a real friend. So I lean into the mirror and look myself in the eyes, and I ask, as gently as I can, "Hey, Daniel, it's okay ... are you?" And I look back at myself and for the first time I think ... maybe? Maybe. Maybe.

Beat.

Yes. Yes yes yes yes yes yes yes yes yes yes yes yes, I'm pretty sure I am, yes. It's like a door gets kicked open in the back of my head and all these thoughts come rushing through— Yes, there were a few boys I was crushing on. Yes I thought some guys were hot (none of the guys at my school because weirdly I seem to have been blessed with not finding douchebags hot—a gift I wish I could share with half the girls I know). Yes I wanted to have a boyfriend, oh my god sooo, sooo bad. Yes I wanted love. I wanted to be loved. I wanted to love. WHO DOESN'T WANT THAT?

Beat.

It's just the way I am. Okay then, but still ... WHAT DOES THAT HAVE TO DO WITH ANYONE ELSE? WHY DOES THAT MAKE PEOPLE SO MEAN? Well. Screw those guys then. Those guys can suck a bag of dicks. Am I right? Am I right? Sorry.

Beat.

I'm still standing at the mirror and I get a text. "We saw a faggot get pushed into the lockers. Was it you?" And I replied. Which I'd never done before. Because I never knew what to say. I type out, "I would prefer if you use the word gay. Faggot is a derogatory term for someone with my sexual orientation." Send.

Beat.

Oh. My. God.

Beat.

No response.

Beat.

No more texts.

Beat.

And just like that I became the first openly gay student at Salisbury Collegiate. And by openly gay I don't mean that I was a walking Pride parade or anything, only that I stopped looking at the floor when I walked down the hall, and I stopped hiding. They didn't know what to do. I enjoyed a few weeks of . . . awe—they were in awe. Finally, for the first time in three years, everyone just left me alone.

Beat.

For a while.

JEREMY Boom. Done.

KRYSTINA *(still writing)* Just a sec!

DANIEL I got called into Principal Evans's office. She was concerned that I was "telling everybody I was gay." She warned me that I was too young to commit to such a "lifestyle choice," but if I insisted on doing so, I should be careful about pushing my "orientation" on my fellow students. I was all, "Really? Because they are not careful at all about pushing their orientation in my face . . . all day long." Wow. I found out I had a lot to say, and I wanted to say it. It meant I had to tell my folks. My dad was silent and my mom kept asking me if I was sure—it wasn't great, but it wasn't all bad; they just wanted me to be careful.

   Beat.

   It was all up to me to shut up and be careful, and, I don't know, but that didn't seem right. It honestly didn't feel like something I could do. And actually, why should I?

JEREMY Time's up! What do you got?

KRYSTINA You first.

JEREMY No. I already came up with one.

KRYSTINA Some of these are really bad.

JEREMY I'm counting on that so that I can mock you.

KRYSTINA No mocking. Safe space.

JEREMY   Safe space unless they're really bad. Just go already.

KRYSTINA   Okay so . . . reasons we need this GSA. Number one. Well I, like you . . .

JEREMY   Yeah?

KRYSTINA   I'm embarrassed when I think about Daniel coming out to me. I didn't know what to do. We were at a movie, and when it was over he turns to me and says, "That lead actor is cute." And in my head I was simultaneously "oh my god!" and "of course!" and "what do I say!?"

JEREMY   What did you say?

KRYSTINA   I just kept . . . talking my face off. About nothing. I was trying as hard as I could to pretend it didn't matter, which it didn't, I mean, that he was gay. But it must have been hard for him to say, even if he acted like it wasn't. And I didn't share anything real about myself in return, and I was too scared to even *ask* Daniel a *question*. ABOUT THE IMPORTANT THING HE JUST SHARED. So, yeah, I guess part of the reason I'm starting this club is to, um—

JEREMY   Be less self-absorbed. Got it. Next?

KRYSTINA   I don't want to lose any more friends.

JEREMY   SLAM! I wrote that one too.

DANIEL   There's a word you guys taught me—someone said it the first meeting I was here . . . *heteronormative*. Assuming we're all straight and that straight is the normal. When you first explained it to me, this light went off in my head, like, oh, heteronormative, like making everyone believe that being straight is the best and only thing . . . basically every hour of every day of high school, you mean? I was glad to hear a word for it, and also, it's a big word and makes me feel all smart and queer savvy. Anyway . . . It was coming up to Valentine's Day. And they have this *heteronormative* tradition at Salisbury where, as a fundraiser for student council, guys could purchase a rose to be delivered to a girl that they liked—they could sign their name or do it secretly—anonymously—or whatever. Carmen was on the student council and she pressured Krystina to volunteer at this table in the cafeteria where guys could come up and place their orders. So Krystina made me sit with her. Which was fine. Only once did some guy ask, "You place any orders for your boyfriend, Danny?" and I said, "I would if I had one," and he said, "That's gross," and Krystina said—

   Shift/flashback. DANIEL *and* KRYSTINA *are at the rose-ordering table in the cafeteria.*

KRYSTINA   *(tearing a form)* Oops. Sorry, Steve, you just lost your order.

   They watch Steve walk away. DANIEL *turns to* KRYSTINA *in awe.*

What? That guy's a jerk. No roses for jerks.

DANIEL   That'll disqualify a lot of the student population. Look, he's going over to complain to Carmen.

KRYSTINA   So? If Carmen doesn't like the way I do business she can sit here herself all lunch.

DANIEL   There's Jeremy.

Beat.

KRYSTINA   Yup.

Beat.

This is so stupid.

DANIEL   Yeah.

KRYSTINA   Why is it just the guys?

DANIEL   What do you mean?

KRYSTINA   Why aren't any girls ordering roses for guys?

DANIEL   Seriously? Do you think guys want to get a *rose*?

KRYSTINA   I bet *you* want a rose.

DANIEL   Shut up.

They smile.

KRYSTINA I just think it's . . . sexist.

DANIEL And you would totally die if you got one.

KRYSTINA Shut up.

> *Beat.*

> Here comes Mr. Johnston.

> *DANIEL freezes.*

> Look, he's smiling and waving—

DANIEL Shut up.

KRYSTINA Don't be rude, wave back.

> *He does, muttering under his breath.*

DANIEL Gah.

KRYSTINA You have such a crush on him.

DANIEL Shut up.

KRYSTINA He's cute. I get it. You wanna send him a rose?

DANIEL Oh my god shut up.

KRYSTINA I'll leave you to recover. Watch the table for me. I gotta pee.

She leaves. DANIEL looks around, slightly less comfortable. After a moment JEREMY approaches.

JEREMY   Hey.

DANIEL   Hey.

   Beat.

   What?

JEREMY   How's it going?

DANIEL   Fine. Why?

   Beat.

JEREMY   So, yeah, bro, I need your help.

DANIEL   "Bro"? Oh, yeah?

JEREMY   Just . . . I wanna order a rose.

DANIEL   Krystina'll be right back.

JEREMY   Yeah, no, / can't you—

DANIEL   I'm just keeping her company. I have no official rose-ordering / powers.

JEREMY   'Kay, so—

DANIEL   They don't want the roses turning gay.

JEREMY   Are you gonna make a big deal out of this? 'Cause I just want to order a stupid rose.

DANIEL   For who, Krystina?

>   *Beat.*

Oh-eM-Gee, it's for Krystina.

JEREMY   Uh . . .

DANIEL   That's so sweet. She'll totally love it and die.

JEREMY   I'm gonna barf now.

DANIEL   Don't, just—quick, fill out this form.

>   *He hands JEREMY a form.*

Or, just, write your message and I'll fill out the rest for you.

JEREMY   I want it to be anonymous though.

DANIEL   What? Why?

JEREMY   I don't want to, like, piss her off—

DANIEL   She'll be pissed off if she gets a rose and it's *anonymous.* I guarantee.

JEREMY But what if she doesn't like it, I mean?

DANIEL I have a feeling she'll like it more if she knows it's from you.

JEREMY Yeah?

DANIEL Yeah, *bro*. Seize the day. If I had someone I . . . had any sort of connection with, you wouldn't catch me being all anonymous about it. Man up.

> *JEREMY fills out the form and hands it to DANIEL.*

You gotta put five bucks in the tin . . .

> *JEREMY does.*

See, wasn't so hard.

JEREMY Yeah.

DANIEL Talking to me, I mean.

> *The boys look at each other.*

JEREMY I better split before she comes back.

> *Back to the two separate classrooms.*

DANIEL With Jeremy that day, I caught a glimpse of . . . how it could work—me being at the school, I mean. We were both guys and both different kinds of guys, but we didn't need to be threatened by each other. I don't know. I watched him walking back to his soccer buddies and wondered how much Krystina was gonna freak out when she got his rose.

He smiles.

KRYSTINA   And . . . ?

JEREMY   What?

KRYSTINA   "I don't want to lose any more friends." You said, "SLAM! I wrote that one too!" And then you zoned out.

JEREMY   Oh, yeah, I was just thinking about . . .

DANIEL   But we never made it to Valentine's Day.

KRYSTINA   What?

JEREMY   Nothing, I . . . here, here's what I wrote *(referring to his paper)*—I want to start a club for kids who are gay or queer or whatever because I want to get to know kids who are gay or queer or whatever. If they're anything like Daniel, I wanna get to know them. And even if they're not, if they're dorky or weird or different or whatever, I want to have the chance to be their friend. Because who knows, right, what someone could give you as a friend, right?

KRYSTINA stares at him.

Is that stupid?

KRYSTINA No. So . . . a place to make new friends?

Beat.

JEREMY Gah. Barf. If we write a mission statement like this no one is gonna wanna come to this loser club.

DANIEL One teacher we had, Mr. Johnston—he taught English and drama and he was also our choir teacher. He had a rule, that in his classroom no one was allowed to use derogatory language based on sexual orientation. He said it out loud, and he stuck to it. He smiled; he asked me how I was doing. He treated me like . . . like I wasn't a problem, I was a . . . good kid, you know? He seemed so cool to me. He was confident in what he liked to do, and he wasn't afraid to show he was passionate about stuff, and I could relate to that. And if I wallowed in my loneliness a bit too much, if I complained to Krystina a few too many times that there was no one at Salisbury for me to date, if sat in my room, staying up way too late making Youtube videos and feeling sorry for myself, I could look at Mr. Johnston and think that one day I could be like him. Funny, I didn't even know he was gay, that he had a partner, until after . . .

KRYSTINA You know that girl Josie?

JEREMY Yeah?

KRYSTINA She came up to me the first day back; I was sitting alone out by the bike racks and she starts asking me— how was my summer, how am I holding up? did I still talk to Daniel? *(imitating Josie's dramatics)* And that she just can't ... get ... over ... what ... happened.

JEREMY   Really?

KRYSTINA   Oh, yeah. I was like, "Could be worse, Josie. He could've died, like you all were hoping he would, you know, like when you posted on his wall 'no one likes you, no one would care if you died' "? And she was all, "That wasn't me! They don't know for sure who did that," and I said, "I don't care if it was you or one of your friends, or one of their boyfriends, or whoever—you're not allowed to pretend like you care. Get out of my face before I punch you—"

JEREMY   WHOA—

KRYSTINA   I know, I KNOW, but I was not having it from Josie. Josie, who I saw in the crowd that day, trying to get to the front to get a better view as Daniel was being beat on. You know what she did when I said that? When I threatened her? She started to cry. "That's so mean," she said, "I can't believe you're being so mean ... "

JEREMY   Maybe she'll show up here? What'll you do then?

KRYSTINA shakes her head.

You gonna give people a chance, Krystina, or they gotta be perfect already?

KRYSTINA   Sure. If they own up. If they apologize.

JEREMY   Okay. Good luck with that.

KRYSTINA   Exactly.

JEREMY   I'm just saying, maybe they act the way they do
            because they don't know another way. And we could
            maybe get them to think about stuff differently, but
            you have to give them a chance—

KRYSTINA   Are you really saying that, Jeremy!? Think about that
            day, okay? Just for a second and then . . . look at me
            and say that again—

DANIEL   It was the weekend before Valentine's Day. Someone
            sent out a picture, and by Monday morning it was on
            everyone's phone. I was wondering why people kept
            asking me if I was looking forward to choir practice
            with Mr. Johnston, and would I be staying after school
            for some one-on-one—

            A shift/flashback. KRYSTINA and DANIEL.

            Let me see it.

KRYSTINA   It's stupid, you don't want to see it.

DANIEL   What is it though? Tell me what it is.

KRYSTINA   It's just a . . . gross picture, it doesn't even look real.

DANIEL   What does it have to do with Mr. Johnston?

            Beat.

Krystina!

KRYSTINA It's . . . it's fake. Photoshopped. You and him. I erased it right away. It's disgusting.

DANIEL Who sent it?

KRYSTINA Brianna, but she didn't make it—

DANIEL WHO MADE IT??

KRYSTINA I don't know, it's being passed around.

> *DANIEL's phone chimes.*

Don't look at it.

> *DANIEL looks at his phone. He stares and stares and stares.*

I'm sorry.

> *JEREMY joins them. He looks over his shoulder to see if anyone's watching, and then he says—*

JEREMY Hey guys. Um . . . just a heads-up, there's a whole bunch of people waiting for Daniel to come out the doors there—

KRYSTINA Why?

JEREMY They wanna, um . . .

DANIEL   They wanna see my face.

KRYSTINA   What do you want to do, Daniel?

DANIEL   I want to die, what do you think?

DANIEL stares out.

JEREMY   Go out the back. Just run.

DANIEL   And tomorrow?

JEREMY   Skip school. It'll blow over.

DANIEL   It'll never blow over.

They wait.

KRYSTINA   Daniel?

DANIEL   Stay here. Don't follow. See you guys on the other side.

DANIEL pushes through the double doors. KRYS-TINA and JEREMY watch him go. DANIEL is back in his classroom in the present, telling the story to us, as KRYSTINA and JEREMY remain in the flashback, watching DANIEL through the double doors.

I push through the double doors out onto the front yard . . . And the crowd parts. To let me through.

JEREMY   It's okay. He's gonna be okay.

DANIEL   I manage to hold my head up. Takes everything in me. And I walk through them. In silence. Until someone says, "Nice picture, Danny." Some whistles and cheers. And . . . I don't think I've given them what they want, and so one of them, this little dude from Jeremy's team, gets in my face so that I actually can't move forward without . . . I have a quick moment where I decide: *eff* this, it's gonna happen anyway, so I shoulder into him to try and get past, and that's it, that's the cue . . . I get pushed down—

KRYSTINA   Oh my god.

DANIEL   —and I try to get up and I'm tripped. And so I swing with my backpack, and then I'm punched / once, twice, and then I'm crawling along the concrete, getting scraped up and just trying to get through, but with blood covering my eye . . .

KRYSTINA   Jeremy! Oh my god! Do something! . . . DO / SOMETHING! GO GET SOMEONE! NOW!

JEREMY   Okay, okay, okay, okay, OKAY!

   KRYSTINA pushes him away and goes through the doors—

KRYSTINA   LEAVE HIM ALONE!

DANIEL   I can hear, somewhere, Krystina screaming, and I look up to see, standing there . . . Mr. Johnston. He picks me up off the ground. And I'm thinking . . . it's official:

God hates me. If I thought anyone, or anything, was looking out for me, I was wrong.

KRYSTINA and JEREMY are back in their classroom in the present. KRYSTINA moves away to be on her own, looking out the door. JEREMY sits.

I went home and I told my folks I fell off my bike, and I went to my room and I didn't come out. And the next day I skipped school. I told my parents I was sick. Only the school called my mom at her work. They told her there'd been some trouble and that a teacher had witnessed me "in a fight."

Beat.

And so my mom comes home from work and sits at the end of my bed and takes my hand and asks me to just tell her what's going on. She says to just talk, that she won't interrupt or question and that whatever I say I won't be in trouble and I can just talk as if she's not there, and say what's on my mind. And I'm thinking, wow . . . my mom is awesome, she's doing absolutely everything right in this situation; it's too bad really, 'cause those kids have totally screwed us, screwed this . . . no way can I tell my mom that someone photoshopped me having an explicit sexual act with my male teacher. I don't care, there is no . . . way. I'm sorry. But they win. They win they win they win they win. They win.

KRYSTINA   And then, when he didn't show up at school, people were being so gross, remember? Guys were high-fiving in the hallway like they were congratulating each other on getting rid of the homo, and their stupid girl-friends would giggle about it. You want me to give *them* a chance? I hate them all, Jeremy. I can't stand it.

JEREMY   You don't hate me, do you?

KRYSTINA   You're not like them.

JEREMY   Don't be so sure.

KRYSTINA   What do you mean?

JEREMY   I just don't know if . . . if I hadn't been part of your study group, if I hadn't had a chance to get to know him, on another level, if . . .

KRYSTINA   What?

JEREMY   I can't say for sure that I wouldn't have been out there, with them, that day.

KRYSTINA   Don't be stupid.

Beat.

JEREMY   There was this one lunch hour, in the caf, and I was showing the guys this funny video on my phone . . .

KRYSTINA   So?

JEREMY   And yeah, and Doug was like, can I see that? And I notice he starts scrolling, looking at other stuff and he says, "You got Daniel's number?" And I said, "It's for class. We're doing a project. So?" and I grab it out of his hand.

KRYSTINA   Doug?

JEREMY   Yeah.

KRYSTINA   The little guy on your team? The one you guys are always laughing at?

JEREMY   "Tiny." Yeah. So the next day I'm in the locker room after practice and I come back from the shower and the guys are gathered around my school bag, and they've got my phone and they're doing something with it. There was this phase when we all would, like, take pics of our butts with each other's phones, so that you find it later and it's, like, a gross surprise—

KRYSTINA   Amazing.

JEREMY   I thought maybe that's what they were trying to do. I didn't think about it. Until way, way later, and . . . I should've figured it out. They were getting his number. For that texting game. They got it from me. And when I did figure it out, I didn't call them on it. It wasn't like it was just any one of them, anyway, right? I mean they shared it out, and shared it out—

KRYSTINA   Shut up, Jeremy. I need a minute.

They sit there.

DANIEL   I go back to school a week later. In a fog. Just flatlined inside. But I didn't stay. I started skipping regularly, which is so not me; I am not that kid. My parents freaked out. Principal Evans talks to me. She sets me up with a counsellor who works with the school and we talk. I didn't know if I was skipping school because I was depressed or because I was afraid and raw, you know? It's the opposite of what they always say, that you learn to deal with these things and it makes you stronger. You toughen up, and then you are better able to live your life, out there in the . . . real world. That hasn't been my experience. I didn't toughen up, I . . . just deadened inside, and then swung wildly from panic to dread to feeling nothing. Panic, dread, nothing. I spent a lot of time thinking . . . "who cares." I had appointments with the counsellor once a week. She gave me assignments, stuff to write about, my feelings. I saw a doctor who put me on antidepressants. I did what everybody said, but I didn't feel better. They were all trying, and it wasn't working. And that made me feel stupid and ashamed, like, *what's wrong with me*!? So I got really good at faking it. But I still had to go into that school every day. I didn't want this person's life, whosoever it was. That feeling that the world hates me and I want to die, that feeling was hanging around. I think that that feeling had actually been there for a while, like, since those early days when people started playing that game, the one where they'd ask, are you a . . . That feeling had been waiting for me to just give into it. So I guess I did. I . . . couldn't help it, I don't think. I gave in.

JEREMY   I'm sorry. I really am.

> *KRYSTINA won't look at him.*

But it's not simple, okay? We're not all like you—like, for whatever reason, you're on top of these things, you think about stuff, and that's great, but the rest of us *screw up. A lot.*

KRYSTINA   No kidding.

JEREMY   Doesn't mean we're happy with the way things go. Or that we don't want something different.

DANIEL   It's not like I didn't have encouragement. I'd become the human trash can for people's . . . I don't even know what to call it. What do you call it when a kid writes anonymous posts like, "You should just do us all a favour and kill yourself." Or, "You should just kill yourself, faggot." Or, on my locker, "No one will ever love you." Or, "You make everyone sick. No one would miss you." Mr. Johnston wouldn't look at me, stopped talking to me at all. Later, after everything, he apologized to my mom: he was afraid of making things worse for me. He'd seen the picture. That's what I finally realized. And when I realized that I . . . threw up. No joke. Not only my own life was garbage, it was spreading, to people who reached out to me. If I had been asked to imagine hell . . . it wouldn't have come close to Salisbury Collegiate. I wrote a note, which said goodbye to everyone, and carried it around in my pocket for a month.

Long beat.

And then one day, it was just the day to do it. I . . . I fully fully fully fully fully fully fully acknowledge now that it was NOT the right thing to do, to try, I . . . when I was in it, it was all I could see. It's an awful place. I wouldn't wish it on anyone, not even those guys who . . . And if I could, I would go to all the kids who are there right now, or who are getting there, and just take them and say, "No, no, here, come here, I know you don't believe me but there's a way out, please please please don't do this." I would go back and do that for myself.

Beat.

Is it okay that I'm talking about this? I don't want to upset anyone. Or maybe I do. We should be upset, I think. We should maybe all be a little more upset about this than we are . . .

KRYSTINA After we heard that Daniel had tried to . . .

JEREMY Yeah.

KRYSTINA And they called that assembly?

JEREMY Yeah.

KRYSTINA I realized then that you were the only one at the school I felt connected to at all.

JEREMY Yeah?

KRYSTINA   I thought, maybe, it was gonna be okay, you know? Daniel hadn't died and so we caught it in time. The teachers and the principal would talk to us and maybe even the cops would come and scare everyone and people would realize that . . . this is real, the stuff we do is real.

JEREMY   Yeah.

KRYSTINA   But then we're at the assembly, and they're talking to us in this really soft manner, and telling us that we *can't blame ourselves*, Daniel wasn't well, and they'd like to take some time to talk to us about suicide prevention and mental-health issues. I was like—

JEREMY   You got so red I thought you were going to explode.

KRYSTINA   I would've if you hadn't held my hand . . .

JEREMY   Yeah. So . . .

KRYSTINA   I had to go from that "prevention assembly" to my friend, in the hospital.

> *Shift/flashback.* KRYSTINA *and* DANIEL *at the hospital.*

You're an idiot.

DANIEL   I beg them to let you visit me and that's the greeting I get?

KRYSTINA   I meant to say something nicer, I swear to god, but . . .

She hugs him, starts to cry.

Dammit, I wasn't going to do that either.

DANIEL   Hi, Krystina.

KRYSTINA   Hi, best friend. Thanks for screwing up and not dying. Also . . . I'm so, so sorry that you—

DANIEL   It's okay. You don't have to say anything.

KRYSTINA   Jeremy says hi.

DANIEL   Cool.

Beat.

KRYSTINA   They treating you nice here?

DANIEL   Oh yeah, it's super sweet.

Beat.

What am I missing?

KRYSTINA   Nothing much. Same old stupid school.

DANIEL   How's Mr. Johnston?

Beat.

KRYSTINA   He's gone. On leave.

Beat.

You can't come back to our school. Okay?

DANIEL   I know. They're working on moving me to a different school. My parents and someone from the board. There's one downtown that has, like, special support for freaks like me—

KRYSTINA   You're not a freak.

DANIEL   So they tell me.

KRYSTINA   Is it a nice school?

DANIEL   Can it be any worse than Salisbury?

KRYSTINA   Um . . . nope.

They sort of laugh. Beat.

DANIEL   I'm sorry.

They look at each other. KRYSTINA can't speak.

I scared the crap out of myself.

Beat.

KRYSTINA   Us too.

Long beat.

DANIEL   And my dad won't stop crying.

Back to the separate classrooms.

Once they had stabilized me, at the hospital, I was sent to psychiatric care and a doctor talked to me, and I told her, finally, everything I've told you so far, pretty much. And while I was telling her the, I don't know, the fact that I was so far away from my school and my home . . . my problems seemed like . . . You know, I once had a weird conversation with Mr. Mercer. He held me back one day after class. "Whatever problems you're having, Daniel, remember to keep some perspective. High school's not everything." And I said, "You mean, it gets better?" And he said, "No, it already is, if you expand your area of thinking. Make your world a little larger than this school and the problems in the school shrink." Sure.

Beat.

Sure.

Beat.

Perspective, eh? Well, why is that my job? Why is it up to me to think bigger? What about the kids who left messages suggesting that I kill myself? What about those kids who spent I don't know how long on their computer photoshopping a picture of me—it seems to me they could use some perspective too, don't you think? You know that when you make that photo, when you write those words, you can't take that shit back. You will always be that person who said those things. Go to the washroom and stand and look in the mirror like I had to, and then see that person in the larger picture of your school, your neighbourhood, your town . . . the country, the world . . .

KRYSTINA *(whispering)* She's back!

JEREMY Our friend?

KRYSTINA Yes!

JEREMY Let me try this time.

> *KRYSTINA moves aside. He goes to the door, speaks out to the girl.*

S'up?

KRYSTINA *(to JEREMY, hushed)* "S'up"!?

JEREMY *(ignoring her, to girl)* You wanna come hang? We are so not going to ask you anything that you don't wanna answer, 'cause we are so . . . down with . . . stuff.

KRYSTINA Oh my god.

JEREMY Oh, okay then. Um . . . later.

> *He turns back to KRYSTINA.*

I'm sorry I made fun of you.

KRYSTINA She's gone?

JEREMY I made her run away. Run. Away.

KRYSTINA What's so scary about us?

JEREMY I don't know. Maybe she'll come in next week.

KRYSTINA We're really gonna keep meeting even if it's just you and me?

JEREMY Well, yeah. What if she hangs around for weeks, working up the courage, and then when she finally decides today's the day we've packed it in?

DANIEL To think you guys were just one district over. With your QSA and your Pride posters in the hall, and you, Ms. Franjelica, and . . . I'm really grateful. You have no idea. I am more than grateful to be here.

Beat.

But I would rather not have to be. I would rather be at my school, my high school, like any other kid. I would rather . . . not have seen my mom and dad look at me the way they did at the hospital when I was recovering, so afraid, and me thinking . . . it'll never be the same, this I can't undo. I . . .

He can't continue . . . He breaks off, exhales—

JEREMY So, what about our mission statement, then?

KRYSTINA   We'll settle on it next meeting.

The bell. She starts to take the banner down.

JEREMY   More people will come. I got a feeling . . .

KRYSTINA   Sure. We'll have pizza. Or something.

JEREMY   That's a great idea.

DANIEL   But anyway, about that favour. I'm putting together a package for Krystina and Jeremy. For support. I was wondering if you guys might sign this card, it says, "We are with you"? So that maybe, if there's not a lot of . . . people there at first, and they're feeling a little lonely or scared or whatever, they can pull this out and look at your signatures and stuff and get some . . . perspective.

The banner is down. KRYSTINA folds it.

JEREMY   I gotta run. Catch you later.

KRYSTINA   Sure, Jeremy. Thanks.

JEREMY scoots off. KRYSTINA turns at the door and stares at the empty room.

DANIEL   What do you guys think?

End of play.

ACKNOWLEDGEMENTS

I am grateful to the following individuals and organizations for their contributions to the development of *Outside*: Kitsilano Secondary School QSA, Spencer Harrison and Georges Vanier Secondary School GSA, Steven Solomon, Jessica Greenberg, PFLAG, Egale, the 519 Community Centre, Buddies in Bad Times Theatre and Roseneath Theatre. I especially thank Andrew, Kyle, Mina, Youness, Giacomo, Maureen, Meghan and Krista for their courage, insight and dedication; Michael, Lindsay and Verne for their artistry and craft; Gretel, Natalie, Heather, Niki, Nan, Katya, Victoria, Brittany, Jim, Annemieke, Courtney and Nicole for working so hard to bring this story into our schools; Rosemary for her guidance and encouragement; and Mark for his love and support.

Paul Dunn is a playwright based in Stratford, Ontario. His plays have been produced by Theatre Direct (*BOYS*), the Stratford Festival (*High-Gravel-Blind*), Studio 180 Theatre (*Offensive Shadows*—Audience Choice Award, SummerWorks Festival), cart/horse theatre (*Dalton and Company*), and Roseneath Theatre (*Outside*—Dora Award Nomination, Outstanding New Play, TYA). He co-authored *The Gay Heritage Project*, which was produced by Buddies in Bad Times Theatre, toured nationally, and was nominated for a Dora Award for Outstanding New Play. His play *Memorial* received an honourable mention from the Herman Voaden National Playwriting Competition. He is also an actor and has worked in theatres across the country.

First edition: September 2017
Printed and bound in Canada by Marquis Imprimeur, Montreal

Cover illustration and design by Patrick Gray
Author photo © Tim Leyes

202-269 Richmond St. W.
Toronto, ON
M5V 1X1

416.703.0013
info@playwrightscanada.com
www.playwrightscanada.com
@playcanpress

PERMANENT   100%   BIO GAZ ÉNERGIE   Garant des forêts intactes